This
MOUSE ⚙ WORKS
Classics Collection Storybook

belongs to

Shelley Howie

Disney's
The Many Adventures Of
WINNIE
The POOH

CLASSIC STORYBOOK

MOUSE WORKS

Published by Penguin Books Australia Ltd, 1998.
© 1989, 1994, 1997 Disney Enterprises, Inc.
Based on the Pooh stories by A.A.Milne,
© The Pooh Properties Trust

Adapted by Llon King
Illustrated by Atelier Philippe Harchy
Original Edition published in English
by Mouse Works, 500 S. Buena Vista St.,
Burbank, CA 91505, USA
Printed and bound in Hong Kong
0 7214 8724 6

3 5 7 9 10 8 6 4 2

CSRVWP97-11

One fine autumn day, Winnie the Pooh sat on a log in front of his house in the Hundred-Acre Wood. "Think, think, think," said Pooh. He was a bear of very little brain, so thinking was sometimes a bit difficult.

"Where can I get more honey?" Pooh wondered, looking around at all the empty honey pots. Then suddenly a bee buzzed by Pooh's nose.

"That buzzing means something," said Pooh. "I think it means you're a bee, and if I were a bee, I'd have honey." This gave Pooh an idea.

"Honey is the best food for a bear!" said Pooh. He
followed the buzzing bee to a tall tree in the forest.
The bee flew up high and disappeared into a big hole—
a honeybee hole.

Pooh ambled over to the tree and began to climb.
"I hope they are friendly bees," he said.

6

Pooh climbed out onto a skinny limb
next to the hole. It was quite a high
place for a bear to be.

"Anyone home?" called Pooh.

"Buzzzzz. Buzzzzz. Buzzzzz," answered
the bees, but they didn't come out.

Suddenly Pooh's little branch got very
wiggly. Then it broke with a crack!

"Oh, bother," said Pooh as he tumbled
downward. "I suppose it all comes from
liking honey so much."

Pooh bounced down the tree from branch to branch, bumping and thinking, thinking and bumping, all the way to the ground.

"It would be much easier if bees lived on the ground," thought Pooh as he fell.

Pooh landed with a thud. "Oh, dear, I'm still quite hungry! Maybe Christopher Robin will know what to do!"

8

Christopher Robin was Pooh's special friend. He just happened to be in the Hundred-Acre Wood with Kanga, Roo, Owl, and Eeyore when he saw the little bear approaching.

"Hello, Pooh!" shouted Christopher Robin.

Pooh ambled over to Christopher Robin and his friends. "I was wondering," said Pooh, "do you have such a thing as a balloon?"

"Whatever for?" asked Christopher Robin.

"Well," Pooh whispered so the bees wouldn't hear, "I'd like to get some honey."

"You don't get honey with a balloon," said his friend.

"Well, I do," said Pooh as he rubbed his tummy. "If I floated past a honeybee tree while hanging onto that balloon, wouldn't I look just like a little cloud floating by? To a bee, I mean?"

"You don't look much like a cloud," said Christopher Robin.

"What if I rolled in a mud puddle and got all dark and muddy?" asked Pooh. "I might look just like a small, black rain cloud...to a bee, of course. And if you had an umbrella and said that it looked like rain—that would fool them for sure."

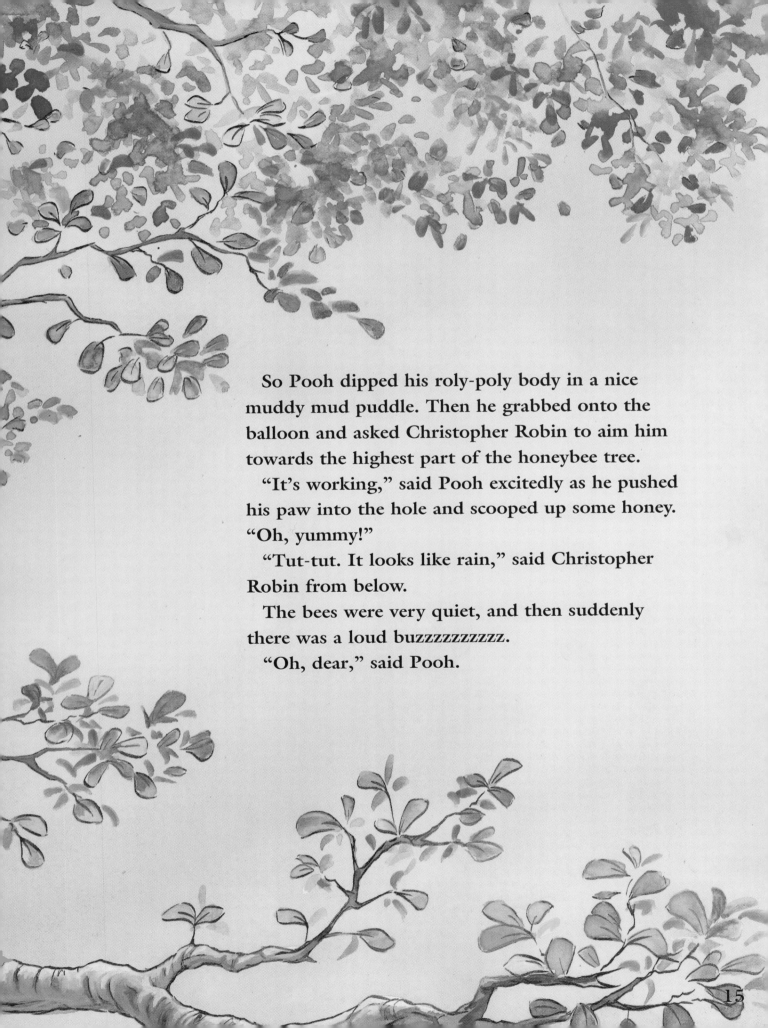

So Pooh dipped his roly-poly body in a nice muddy mud puddle. Then he grabbed onto the balloon and asked Christopher Robin to aim him towards the highest part of the honeybee tree.

"It's working," said Pooh excitedly as he pushed his paw into the hole and scooped up some honey. "Oh, yummy!"

"Tut-tut. It looks like rain," said Christopher Robin from below.

The bees were very quiet, and then suddenly there was a loud buzzzzzzzzz.

"Oh, dear," said Pooh.

As the bees swarmed around Pooh, the string on the balloon loosened, letting all its air out.

"I think the bees suspect something!" Pooh cried as he went speeding past atop the balloon. There were bees everywhere, chasing poor Pooh.

Finally the balloon ran out of air, and Pooh fell to the ground. "I'll save you, Pooh!" cried Christopher Robin.

"I have never seen so many angry bees," said Christopher Robin. "Hurry, Pooh! Into the mud puddle!"

Christopher Robin opened his umbrella, and the two friends huddled under it. They waited a long time in the dark, sticky mud while the grumpy bees dived down and bounced off the umbrella. Finally the bees flew back to the honey tree.

"Those were not the right sort of bees," said Pooh with a sigh.

"Silly old bear!" laughed Christopher Robin.

Winnie the Pooh didn't give up easily, especially when it came to honey.

"Honey rhymes with bunny!" said Pooh. "I think I'll visit my friend Rabbit. He always has a little snack about this time of day."

Pooh's nose twitched as he stood outside Rabbit's house. "Hello!" Pooh shouted. "Is anybody home?"

"Is that you, Pooh?" asked a reluctant Rabbit from inside. "Oh, dear. It is you. Well, come in, Pooh. I'm just having a little snack of bread and…honey."

"Would you like some honey on your bread?" asked Rabbit after he let Pooh in.

"Never mind about the bread. I'll just take a small helping of honey," said Pooh with a smile.

And so Pooh began to eat. And he ate and ate and ate...until Rabbit had no honey left.

"You'll be going now, I suppose," said Rabbit quietly as he watched Pooh lick the last bit from the last honey pot.

"Thank you, Rabbit," said Pooh, smiling. "That was delicious. You are a very good friend. Good-bye."

Pooh pushed himself into the hole that was the doorway to Rabbit's house. But he didn't get far.

"Oh, oh, oh, help and bother! I'm stuck," said Pooh. But no matter how hard Rabbit pushed or pulled, Pooh didn't budge, not even one inch.

"It all comes from eating too much honey!" said Rabbit. He gave Pooh a final, big push from behind. But it didn't work. Pooh was a very stuck bear.

Rabbit ran out his back door and got Christopher Robin.
But even Christopher Robin could not unstick poor Pooh.

"Pooh Bear, there's only one thing we can do—wait for you
to get thin again," Christopher Robin finally said.

"How long will that take?" asked Pooh.

"Days. Weeks. Months. Who knows?" replied Rabbit.

"Don't worry, Pooh," said Christopher Robin as he left with
Rabbit. "I'll get some help. We'll get you out sooner than that."

Soon Gopher, the excavation expert, arrived at the scene. "What's the problem?" he asked.

"I'm stuck in Rabbit's doorway, and I can't get unstuck," sighed Pooh.

"Whew!" Gopher whistled. "Gophers know how to dig, but gophers don't know anything about getting bears out of holes." Gopher opened his lunch box. "Care for some honey?"

"Oh, no! Not that!" cried Rabbit, racing out of his house. "Don't feed the bear! Not one drop!"

You see, Rabbit was getting tired of having part of Pooh in his living room.

Finally one morning, Pooh budged. Christopher Robin
came back with all of Pooh's friends.

"Maybe we can all try pulling together," Christopher
Robin said.

"Please hurry," said Pooh. "This hole is tight, and I'm
getting hungry."

Eeyore pulled on Kanga. Kanga pulled on Christopher
Robin. Christopher Robin pulled as hard as he could.
But Pooh was too stuck.

The others were pulling as hard as they could outside Rabbit's house. Inside his house, Rabbit aimed his head and got ready to run. Picking up speed, he smashed into Pooh's backside, pushing with all his might.

Pop! Pooh shot right out of Rabbit's front door and flew up into the sky like a rocket.

"There he goes!" shouted Kanga.

"He's sailing!" shouted Rabbit.

"Watch out!" yelled Christopher Robin as Pooh sailed towards a big tree.

"I'm trying to watch out," hollered Pooh. His head and shoulders disappeared right into another hole—this one high up in the tree.

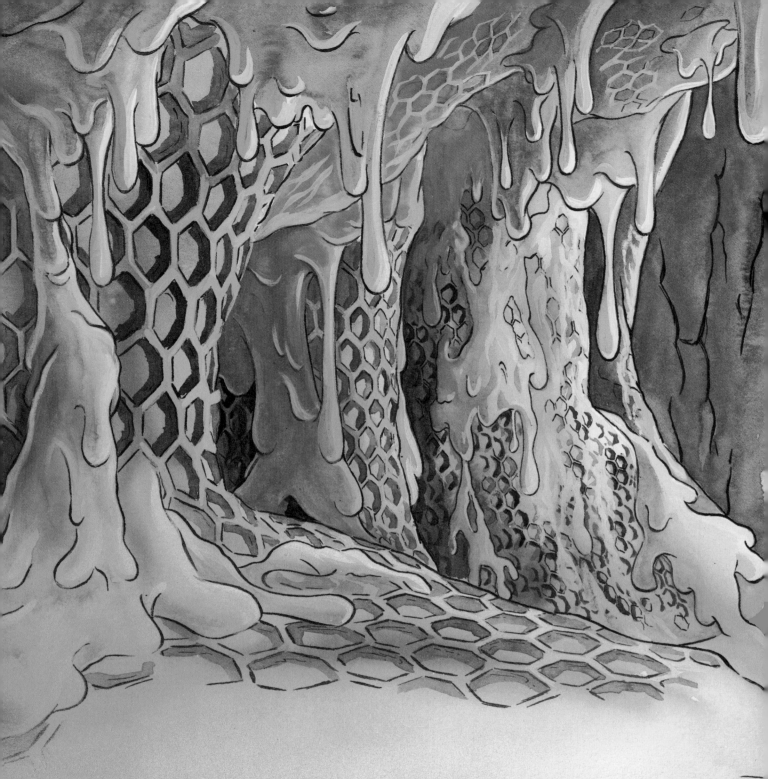

But Pooh was not at all unhappy. The hole where he had landed was full of honey!

"Don't worry, Pooh. We'll get you out!" Christopher Robin cried.

"No hurry," Pooh yelled back. "Take your time." Then he laughed and sang as he dipped his paws into the golden honey. 🐝

Piglet was one of Pooh's best friends. He lived in a fine old tree in the Hundred-Acre Wood. One blustery autumn day, Piglet was sweeping up leaves in front of his door. No matter how hard Piglet swept, the wind blew back more leaves. It was a big wind—a blustery, busy autumn wind.

"Oh, d-d-dear!" worried Piglet. "I'll never finish sweeping these leaves before my friend Pooh arrives."

Suddenly the wind got even bigger. It lifted Piglet right up off the ground.

39

Piglet sailed over Pooh's head.

"Hello, Piglet!" said the surprised Pooh. "I was just coming to visit you. Where are you going?"

"That's what I want to know, t-t-too," said Piglet as he sailed by.

Pooh managed to grab hold of Piglet's scarf. It began to unravel as the wind pulled Pooh along, but Pooh held the thread tightly.

"Mama!" cried Roo. "Look at the funny kite!"

"Oh, my goodness!" said Kanga. "That's not a kite. It's Piglet! Hang on, Pooh!" yelled Kanga.

"Hang on, Piglet!" yelled Roo.

And the wind just got bigger and whooshier.

The wind got so big it lifted Pooh right off the ground. But Pooh held on tightly to the thread from Piglet's scarf.

There was a giant old tree in front of them. And in the tree there was a house.

"Pooh, w-w-where does the wind blow things?" asked Piglet.

"I don't know," answered Pooh bravely. "That's what we're about to find out."

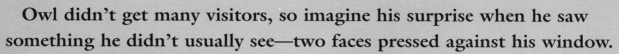

Owl didn't get many visitors, so imagine his surprise when he saw something he didn't usually see—two faces pressed against his window.

"Who-who-who is there?" asked Owl politely.

"It's m-m-me," said Piglet.

"And me, too," said Pooh. "We were passing by, and we just dropped in."

"Amazing!" exclaimed Owl. "Don't you know it's windy out there? You had better come inside!"

Owl was pleased to have visitors, and he offered his friends honey and tea. "Your visit," said Owl, "reminds me so very much of the Great Windstorm of '67. That was the year my great-aunt Clara traveled to—"

Owl didn't get to finish his story. The wind blew up a sudden, terrific, powerful gust. And the whole tree house began to tip to one side.

Owl's house crashed to the ground with everyone still inside. Christopher Robin, Rabbit, and Eeyore hurried over to see if they could help.

"Don't worry, Owl," said Christopher Robin. "We'll find you a new house."

"We sure will," said all the friends. And eventually they did.

It had been a long day for Pooh. He snuggled cozily in his bed, ready for sleep. But the wind was still blowing, and the night was full of strange noises. There was one noise that Pooh had never heard before. It was just outside his door.

"Grrrr!" went the noise.

"P-P-Piglet?" asked Pooh, shivering a little. "Is that you?" But "Grrrr!" was still the only sound that Pooh heard. Pooh went to the door to investigate.

Suddenly a large orange creature with black stripes bounced right on top of Pooh, knocking him over.

"Hoo-hoo-hoo! I'm Tigger," said the creature, looking down at Pooh.

"My name is Pooh. And you scared me!" Pooh answered.

"Of course I scared ya. Tiggers are supposed ta be scary," replied Tigger. But he wasn't very scary, really.

"I don't think I've seen a tigger before," said Pooh. "What does a tigger do?"

"Why, tiggers bounce!" said Tigger loudly. And he bounced all around the room. "Nothing can bounce like a tigger. Tiggers are wonderful things!" he said. "Be on guard!" shouted Tigger as he bounced towards the door. "There are things in the forest tonight, strange things."

"What sort of strange things?" asked Pooh.

"Why, heffalumps and woozles, of course!" yelled Tigger. "Be on guard. They like honey!" And he bounced right out the door.

Pooh wanted to stay awake and keep watch for heffalumps and woozles or any other creatures that might be interested in his honey, but he was quite tired from watching the bouncing Tigger and from the excitement of the blustery day.

Pooh fell asleep. As Pooh slept, he began to dream. It was a strange dream about honey and heffalumps and woozles. While Pooh was dreaming, it began to rain.

Pooh's dreams were usually about honey. But on this stormy
night, heffalumps and woozles floated into his dream.

In the dream, a giant heffalump grabbed Pooh's best honey pot
and began to fly away. Pooh chased after his honey pot, trying to
save it.

"Come back! Come back!" yelled Pooh.

Pooh awoke with a start. The heffalumps and woozles were gone. But his house was full of water!

"Oh, no! My honey!" shouted Pooh. "I mustn't let the water get inside my honey pots!"

He quickly gathered them up and carried them outside. The water was rising higher and higher in the Hundred-Acre Wood.

Pooh put the honey pots on the branch of a tree where they would
be safe. As he was arranging them, he saw Piglet float by on a chair.
"Are you all right, Piglet?" asked Pooh.
"H-h-help me, Pooh," his little friend answered as he floated by.

Before he floated out of his house, Piglet had managed to send a message in a bottle. His message was soon found, and Piglet's friends spread out to search for him. Owl was the first to spot him. He saw Piglet right away.

"Don't worry, Piglet," Owl called. "We'll soon have you out."

Pooh was harder to see because he had his head stuck in a honey pot, but Owl spotted him, too.

As Owl flew above them, Pooh and Piglet drifted over a very big waterfall indeed. When they reached the bottom, Pooh was on Piglet's chair, and Piglet was in Pooh's honey pot.

When they finally reached dry land—and the rest of their friends—Christopher Robin looked at Piglet floating safely in Pooh's honey pot.

"Pooh, you are a hero!" said Christopher Robin.

"Let's celebrate!" said Christopher Robin. "Let's have a hero party!"

"Great idea!" cheered the friends.

Christopher Robin hurried to get hats and flags and napkins. "What sort of cake would you like, Pooh?" asked Christopher Robin.

"Well," Pooh said, "if it's all the same to you, I'll just have some…"

"Honey!" everyone shouted, and they laughed all at once.

A few weeks later, Rabbit was out picking carrots in his garden. "Halloooo!" called Tigger as he bounced through the garden, upsetting Rabbit's plants.

"Look out!" cried Rabbit. "My garden! Tigger, can't you stop bouncing just for one minute? Look what you did to my garden," he sputtered. "You ruined it. And you are standing on top of me!"

"Ooops. Sorry about that," said Tigger. "But tiggers can't stop bouncing. Bouncing's what tiggers do best!"

Early the next morning Pooh, Piglet, and Tigger met Rabbit in the woods. As usual, Tigger bounced ahead of everybody.

"Listen," whispered Rabbit, "I have a plan. We're going to teach Tigger a lesson to scare the bounce out of him. We'll take him deep into the woods and then we'll lose him. Quick! Follow me."

"Let's hide in this old tree trunk," whispered Rabbit.

"What about Tigger?" said Piglet. "This will be scary for him." Pooh looked worried, too.

"Oh, don't worry!" Rabbit whispered back. "We are going to lose Tigger just for tonight. We'll find him again in the morning."

"Halloo!" shouted Tigger. "Where is everybody?" Tigger looked up and down and back and forth. Then he scratched his head and bounced off into the woods.

After Tigger had bounced out of sight, the three friends started towards home. But the woods looked different in the thick mist.

"Excuse me, Rabbit," Pooh said quietly. "I think we're going in circles. We keep ending up at this same pit."

"We're not going in circles!" Rabbit declared confidently. "That's ridiculous. We can't be lost. Tigger is the one who is lost, remember?"

Pooh and Piglet were too tired to remember.

"You wait here," Rabbit said. "I'll walk away from this pit, and if I don't come back, that proves we are not going in circles."

Pooh and Piglet found their way home easily after a little sleep. Pooh followed his tummy to his honey pots. When it came to honey, Pooh's tummy never got lost.

But Rabbit was still wandering around lost in the mist. He was a very scared rabbit now. All around he heard frightening noises.

"Grrrr! Grrrrup!" said the noises.

"Help!" wailed Rabbit. "Piglet! Pooh! Somebody! Oh, please help me!"

Suddenly Tigger came bouncing out of the mist. "Halloo, Rabbit!"
"Tigger!" cried Rabbit. "But—but—you're supposed to be lost."
"Tiggers never get lost, bunny boy," Tigger exclaimed. "Never!
Come on! Grab my tail. I'll bounce ya outta here."
    And Tigger bounced a very humble and quiet Rabbit all the
way home.

When the first snowfall covered the Hundred-Acre Wood, Tigger took Roo out to play. Roo loved Tigger because Tigger was fun. He bounced and laughed. He was brave. Tigger could do anything! Roo pointed to a tall oak tree up ahead. "Look at that tree, Tigger! I bet you could climb that tall, tall tree in just five bounces!"

"No problem," replied Tigger. "Bouncing's what tiggers do best!" And Tigger bounced up the tree, right to the top.

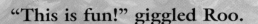

"This is fun!" giggled Roo.

But at the top, Tigger did something tiggers don't often do. He looked down at the ground. "Oh, no," said Tigger. "I forgot one important thing about tiggers."

"What did you forget?" laughed Roo, as he swung on Tigger's tail.

"I forgot that tiggers don't climb trees." Tigger looked down again. "How did this tree get so high?" Tigger held onto the tree trunk as tightly as he could. "Please don't swing on my tail, Roo," he said nervously. "You're shaking the tree."

Roo let go of Tigger's tail and landed on a lower branch. Just then Tigger saw Pooh and Piglet, who had come out to play in the snow. But Pooh and Piglet didn't see him. "Halloooo! Halloooo!" Tigger shouted, startling his friends with his booming voice.

"Oh, look, Piglet—it's Tigger and Roo," said Pooh.

"What are you doing up in that t-t-tree?" asked Piglet.

"I'm all right," said Roo. "But Tigger is stuck."

It wasn't long before word got back to Christopher Robin and the others that Tigger and Roo were in trouble. "I know what we can do," said Christopher Robin. He took off his winter coat. Pooh, Kanga, and Piglet each grabbed a corner.

"Jump!" Christopher Robin yelled to Roo. "We'll catch you."

"And try not to fall too fast, dear," said Kanga.

"Here I come!" laughed Roo. "Wheeee!" Roo bounced into Christopher Robin's warm coat. "Gee, that was fun!" he said.

"You're next, Tigger," Christopher Robin yelled.

"Come on, Tigger. Jump!" shouted Roo.

"Jump?! Tiggers don't jump. They bounce!" said Tigger, holding on tightly.

Christopher Robin laughed. "Well, then—bounce," he said. "Bounce down, Tigger. We'll catch you."

"Don't be ridiculous," said Tigger. "Tiggers don't bounce down. Tiggers only bounce up." And he held on even tighter.

"Well, then," said Rabbit from below, "I guess you'll have to stay up there forever."

"Forever?" asked Tigger. Tigger was very unhappy. "Oh, if I get out of this, I promise never to bounce again," said Tigger. "Never!"

Rabbit was thrilled about Tigger's promise not to bounce. He helped Christopher Robin convince Tigger to slide down the tree, one inch at a time.

It took a long time, but Tigger got down.

"I'm so happy, I feel like bouncing!" cried Tigger as soon as he reached the ground.

"Ah-ah-ah," said Rabbit. "You promised never to bounce again."

Tigger remembered. But he looked so sad that everyone—including Rabbit—felt sorry for him.

"Well, I—ah…oh, all right!" Rabbit finally said. "Tigger can have his bounce back."

"Hoo-hoo-hoo! Thank you, Rabbit!" Tigger cried. "Come on! Let's all bounce!"

And so everyone bounced off into the snowy Hundred-Acre Wood, where they shared many more wonderful adventures.

The End